WILDTRACK

AND OTHER STORIES

WILDTRACK

AND OTHER STORIES

ROSE TREMAIN

IMAGES BY
JEFF FISHER

FULL CIRCLE EDITIONS

Also by Rose Tremain

Novels
Sadler's Birthday
Letter to Sister Benedicta
The Cupboard
The Swimming Pool Season
Restoration
Sacred Country
The Way I Found Her
Music & Silence
The Colour
The Road Home
Trespass

Short Story Collections
The Colonel's Daughter
The Garden of the Villa Mollini
Evangelista's Fan
The Darkness of Wallis Simpson

For Children
Journey to the Volcano

Contents

Introduction

I was born in London and spent my childhood there, where bomb sites still blighted large areas of the city and where clothes and sweets were still rationed. In the school holidays, I and my sister were taken to our grandfather's farm in Hampshire and we loved these visits so much, we used to count the days in between.

I was a city kid, then, who pined for the countryside, and in 1976, when my daughter was still a toddler, I moved to a farmhouse in Suffolk and discovered the wide skies and watery byways of East Anglia. Since which time, I've never lived anywhere else. I've moved house, changed partners, but remained faithful to this corner of England, and this is where most of my fiction finds its setting.

In my 1989 novel, *Restoration*, my anti-hero Merivel, when he falls out of favour with King Charles II and is exiled to East Anglia, notices that here, "the landscape became, as it were less and the sky more and the creatures most numerous were the birds, who had their existence in both elements". Merivel is reacting to the changed light and to "the crust of the earth [which] appears thin, allowing water to seep and ooze upwards, so that it is possible to imagine that there are fishes and not worms in the soil". He understands that he's entered a landscape of reflections, where the eye may be deceived and yet is often forced to gaze unflinchingly towards a far-away horizon. It is here, first in the Cambridgeshire fens and then in Norfolk, that Merivel will discover the path towards his own "restoration", and it is here that my storyteller's eye found a place in which it could see more clearly than ever before.

The stories in this small collection were written over a protracted period of time. *A Shooting Season* dates back to 1983. *Peerless* was written in 2006. The other two, *Wildtrack* and *Strawberry Jam,* fit somewhere in between. Reading them again, I felt, at first, that nothing united them except their East Anglian location, which, in every case, is an essential and vivid part of the story. But now I see that the protagonists of three of the four pieces have something else in common: their awareness of something missing or wrong in their day-to-day lives which needs their intervention. Indeed, these three stories exist to discover how that intervention may be achieved.

The exception is *A Shooting Season,* in which the protagonist, Anna, believes she has discovered for herself a sanctuary, where she will be protected from intervention of any kind. The sanctuary is an isolated Norfolk cottage near a weedy river or broad and Anna is at first very happy here, deciding that, like the family of ducks she finds on the water, she has everything she could possibly need, including the fragile beginnings of some new work. Then The Past shows up—as it has a terrible habit of doing in any life—and everything that has been consoling to Anna is consoling no longer.

In *Strawberry Jam* (for which the core idea was gifted to me by a student of mine who felt she could do nothing with it), motherless fourteen year-old Holly becomes convinced that her Austrian neighbours in Suffolk have committed a terrible crime and that she has to be the one to solve the surrounding mystery. Holly's world is very small—defined by the house and garden she shares with her "hippy Dad" on a quiet road "down which nobody travels". So every detail of this world—from the types of fruit trees growing in the gardens to the starchy food Holly and her father eat, from the clothes seen on the neighbours' washing line to the shoes Holly wears at her mother's funeral—is significant. I remember that when I wrote this story, I located it in my mind in the place where I then lived, a Suffolk cottage on the edge of a village, near a small byway "down which nobody travelled". It was the place where my daughter grew up and in which, for the most part, I was very happy. Ever since that time, the sound of an occasional car whispering along such a road—not very near and yet not very far away—has been profoundly consoling to me.

In both *Wildtrack* and *Peerless*, the male protagonists, Micky and Badger, though far apart in age, share a debilitating sense of sad loneliness, connected to the belief that what was important in their lives has gone for ever. The stories relate their efforts to reconnect with the lost things and to find something to hold onto in the future that will give their lives purpose and meaning. This important question, how we find meaning in a secular life, especially after the age of sixty or so, is one which is worthy, I think, of tireless exploration, and I have addressed it again in my new novel, *Trespass* (Chatto, March 2010). Quite often, short stories may prove to be *essais* for larger works of fiction, even though the writer doesn't know this at the time.

Trespass has two locations: London and the hills of the Cévennes in southern France. It's the first of my novels since *The Way I Found Her*, 1995, to have no scene set in East Anglia. But landscape is nevertheless of prime importance in the book. The Cévennes region—unlike Norfolk and Suffolk—is densely forested and tinder-dry in summer, but it shares with East Anglia that abiding sense of a place cut off from the centre, from the hub or nub of the world, a place where the weather shapes people's lives in a significant way, where secrets abound, where the nights are very dark. And it is precisely in such a place that my imagination feels most free and unfettered, where the kinds of stories that are important to me can find a habitation and a name.

Rose Tremain, 2010

Peerless

His parents had christened him Broderick, but for as long as he could remember, he'd always been known as "Badger". He spent his life feeling that Badger was a fatuous name, but he couldn't stand Broderick either. To him, the word "Broderick" described a *thing*—possibly a gardening implement or a DIY tool—rather than a human being. Becoming an animal, he decided, was better than remaining a thing.

Now, because he was getting old, it worried Badger that the hours (which, by now, would have added up to years) he'd spent worrying about these two useless names of his could have been far better spent worrying about something else. The world was in a state. Everybody could see that. The north and south poles, always reliably blue in every atlas, now had flecks of yellow in them. He knew that these flecks were not printers' errors. He often found himself wishing that he had lived in the time of Scott of the Antarctic, when ice was ice. The idea of everything getting hotter and dirtier made Badger Newbold feel faint.

Newbold. That was his other name. "Equally inappropriate," he'd joked to his future wife, Verity, as he and she sat in the crimson darkness of the 400 Club, smoking du Maurier cigarettes. "Not bold. Missed the war. Spend my days going through ledgers and adding up columns. Can't stand mess. Prefer everything to be tickety-boo."

"Badger," Verity had replied, with her dimpled smile, with her curvy lips, red as blood, "you seem bold to me. Nobody has dared to ask me to marry them before!"

She'd been so adorable then, her brown eyes so sparkly and teasing, her arms so enfolding and soft. Badger knew he'd been lucky to get her. If that was the word? If you could "get" another person and make them yours and cement up the leaks where love could escape. If you could do that, then Badger Newbold had been a fortunate man. All his friends told him so. He was seventy now. Verity was sixty-nine. On the question of love, they were silent. Politeness had replaced love.

They lived in a lime-washed farmhouse in Suffolk on the pension Badger had saved, working as an accountant, for thirty-seven years. Their two children, Susan and Martin, had gone off to live their lives in far-off places on the other side of the burning globe: Australia and California. Their mongrel dog, Savage, had recently died and been buried, along with all the other mongrel dogs they'd owned, under a forgiving chestnut tree in the garden. And, these days, Badger found himself very often alone.

He felt that he was waiting for something. Not just for death. In fact, he did nothing much except wait. Verity often asked him in the mornings: "What are you going to do today, Badger?" and it was difficult to answer this. Badger would have liked to be able to reply that he was going to restore the polar ice cap to its former state of atlas blue, but, in truth, he knew perfectly well that his day was going to be empty of all endeavour. So he made things up. He told Verity he was designing a summer house, writing to the children, pruning the viburnum, overhauling the lawnmower or repairing the bird table.

She barely noticed what he did or didn't do. She was seldom at home. She was tearing about the place, busy beyond all reason, trying to put things to rights. She was a volunteer carer at the local Shelter for Battered Wives. She was a Samaritan. Her car was covered with "Boycott Burma" stickers. Her "Stop the War in Iraq" banner—which she held aloft in London for nine hours—was taped to the wall above her desk. She sent half her state pension to Romanian Orphanages, Cancer Research, Greenpeace, Friends of the Earth, Amnesty

International, Victims of Torture and the Sudan Famine Fund. She was never still, always trembling with outrage, yet ready with kindness. Her thick grey hair looked perpetually wild, as though desperate hands had tugged it, in this direction and that. Her shoes were scuffed and worn.

Badger was proud of her. He saw how apathetic English people had become, slumped on their ugly, squashy furniture. Verity was resisting apathy. "Make every day count" was her new motto. She was getting old, but her heart was like a piston, powering her on. When a new road threatened the quiet of the village, it was Verity who had led the residents into battle against the council—and won. She was becoming a local heroine, stunningly shabby. She gave away her green Barbour jacket and replaced it with an old black duffel coat, bought from the Oxfam shop. In this, with her unkempt hair, she looked like a vagrant, and it was difficult for Badger to become reconciled to this. He felt that her altered appearance made him seem stingy.

The other thing which upset Badger about the new Verity was that she'd gone off cooking. She said she couldn't stand to make a fuss about food when a quarter of the world was living on tree bark. So meals, in the Newbold household, now resembled post-war confections: ham and salad, shop-bought cake, rice pudding, jacket potatoes with margarine. Badger felt that it was unfair to ask him to live on these unappetising things. He was getting constipated. He had dreams about Béarnaise sauce. Sometimes, guiltily he took himself to the Plough at lunchtime and ordered steak pie and Guinness and rhubarb crumble. Then he would go home and fall asleep. And in the terror of a twilight awakening, Badger would berate himself for being exactly the kind of person Verity despised: apathetic, self-indulgent and weak. At such times, he began to believe it was high time he went to see his Maker. When he thought about heaven, it resembled the old 400 Club, with shaded pink lights and waiters with white bow ties and music, sad and sweet.

★

One spring morning, alarmingly warm, after Verity had driven off somewhere in her battered burgundy Nissan, Badger opened a brown envelope addressed to him—not to Verity—from a place called the Oaktree Wildlife Sanctuary. It was a home for animals that had been rescued from cruelty or annihilation. Photographs of peacefully grazing donkeys, cows, sheep, geese, chickens and deer fell out from a plastic brochure. Badger picked these up and looked at them. With his dogs, the last Savage included, Badger had felt that he had always been able to tell when the animals were happy. Their brains might be tiny, but they could register delight. Savage had had a kind of grin, seldom seen, but suddenly there in the wake of a long walk, or lying on the hearthrug in the evenings, when the ability to work the CD player suddenly returned to Verity and she would put on a little Mozart. And, looking at these pictures, Badger felt that these animals (and even the birds) were in a state of contentment. Their field looked spacious and green. In the background were sturdy shelters, made of wood.

Inside the brochure was a letter in round writing, which began:

> *Dear Mr Newbold,*
> *I am a penguin and my name is Peerless.*

At this point, Badger reached for his reading glasses, so that he could see the words properly. Had he read the word "Peerless" correctly? Yes, he had. He went on, reading:

> *… I was going to be killed, along with my mates, Peter, Pavlov, Palmer and Pooter, when our zoo was closed down by the Council. Luckily for me, the Oaktree Wildlife Sanctuary stepped in and saved us. They've dug a pond and installed a plastic slide for us. We have great fun there, walking up the slide and slipping down again. We have a good diet of fish. We are very lucky penguins.*
> *However, we do eat quite a lot and sometimes we have to be*

*examined by the vet. All of this cost the Sanctuary a lot of money.
So we're looking for Benefactors. For just £25 a year you could
become my Benefactor. Take a look at my picture. I'm quite smart,
aren't I?*

*I take trouble with my personal grooming. I wasn't named "Peerless"
for nothing. Please say that you will become my Benefactor. Then, you
will be able to come and visit me any time you like. Bring your family.*
With best wishes from Peerless the Penguin.

Badger unclipped the photograph attached to the letter and looked
at Peerless. His bill was yellow, his coat not particularly sleek. He was
standing in mud at the edge of the pond. He looked as though he had
been stationary in that one place for a long time.

Peerless.

Now, Badger laid all the Sanctuary correspondence aside and leaned
back in his armchair. He closed his eyes. His hands covered his face.

★

Peerless had been the name of his friend at boarding school. His only
real friend.

Anthony Peerless. A boy of startling beauty, with a dark brow and
dimpled smile and colour always high, under the soft skin of his face.

He'd been clever and dreamy, useless at cricket, unbearably
homesick for his mother. He'd spent his first year fending off the sixth-
formers, who passed his photograph around until it was chewed and
faded. Then, Badger had arrived and become his friend. And the two
had clung together, Newbold and Peerless, Badger and Anthony, in that
pitiless kraal of a school. Peerless the dreamer, Badger the mathematical
whiz. An unlikely pair.

No friendship had ever been like this one.

"Are you aware, Newbold, that your friend, Peerless, has been late
for games three times in three weeks?"

"No, I wasn't aware, sir."

"Well, now you are. And what do you propose to do about it?"

"I don't know."

"I don't know, sir!"

"I don't know, sir."

"Well, I think I know. You can warn Peerless that if he is ever—ever—late for cricket again, then I , personally, will give you a beating. Do you understand, Newbold? I am making you responsible. If you fail in your task, it will be you who will be punished."

Peerless is in the grounds of the school, reading Keats. Badger sits down by him, among daisies, and says: "I say, old thing, the Ogre's just given me a bit of an ultimatum. He's going to beat me if you're late for cricket practice again."

Peerless looks up and smiles his girlish, beatific smile. He starts picking daisies. He's told Badger he loves the smell of them, like talcum powder, like the way his mother smells.

"The Ogre's mad, Badger. You realize that, don't you?" says Peerless.

"I know," says Badger. "I know."

"Well, then, we're not going to collude with him. Why should we?"

And that's all that can be said about it. Peerless returns to Keats and Badger lies down beside him and asks him to read something aloud.

> *…overhead - look overhead*
> *Among the blossoms white and red.*

★

When Verity came back that evening from wherever she'd been, Badger showed her the photograph of Peerless the Penguin and said: "I'm going to be his Benefactor."

Verity laughed at the picture. "Typical you, Badger!" she snorted.

"Why typical me?"

"Save animals. Let the people go hang."

Badger ate his ham and salad in silence for a while; then he said: "I don't think you've got any idea what you've just said."

There wasn't a moment's pause, not a second's thought, before Verity snapped: 'Yes, I do. You're completely apathetic when it comes to helping people. But where animals are concerned, you'll go to the ends of the bloody earth."

"Perhaps that's because I am one," said Badger. "An animal."

"Oh, shut up, Badger," said Verity. "You really do talk such sentimental bollocks."

Badger got up and walked out of the room. He went out on to the terrace and looked at the spring moon. He felt there was a terrible hunger in him, not just for proper food, but for something else, something which the moon's light might reveal to him, if he stayed there long enough, if he got cold enough, waiting. But nothing was revealed to him. The only thing that happened was that, after ten or fifteen minutes, Verity came out and said: "Sorry Badger. I can be a pig."

★

Badger wrote to Peerless and sent his cheque for £25. An effusive thank-you note arrived, inviting him to visit the Sanctuary.

It wasn't very far away. But Badger's driving was slow, these days, and he frequently forgot which gear he was in. Sometimes, the engine of the car started screaming, as if in pain. It always seemed to take this screaming engine a long time to get him anywhere at all. Badger reflected that if, one day, he was obliged to drive to London, he would probably never manage to arrive.

He drove at last down an avenue of newly planted beeches. Grassy fields lay behind them. At the end of the drive was a sign saying "Welcome to Oaktree Wildlife Sanctuary" and a low red-brick building with a sundial over the door. It was an April day.

At a reception desk, staffed by a woebegone young man with thick glasses, Badger announced himself as the Benefactor of Peerless the Penguin and asked to see the penguin pool.

"Oh, certainly," said the young man, whose name was Kevin. "Do you wish to avail yourself of the free wellingtons service?"

Badger saw ten or eleven pairs of green wellingtons lined up by the door.

He felt that free wellingtons and new beech trees were a sign of something good. "Imagination," Anthony Peerless used to say, "is everything. Without it, the world's doomed."

Badger put on some wellingtons, too large for his feet, and followed the young man across a meadow where donkeys and sheep were grazing. These animals had thick coats and they moved in a slow, unfrightened way.

"Very popular with children, the donkeys," said Kevin. "But they want rides, of course and we don't allow this. These animals have been burdened enough."

"Quite right," said Badger.

And then, there it was, shaded by a solitary oak, a grey pond, bordered by gunnera and stinging nettles. At one end of it was the slide, made of blue plastic, and one of the penguins was making its laborious way up some wide plastic steps to the top of it.

"So human, aren't they?" said Kevin, smiling.

Badger watched the penguin fall forwards and slither down into the muddy water of the pond. Then he asked: "Which one's Peerless?"

Kevin stared short-sightedly at the creatures. His gaze went from one to the other, and Badger could tell that this man didn't know. Someone had given the penguins names, but they resembled each other so closely, they might as well not have bothered. It was impossible to distinguish Pooter from Pavlov, Palmer from Peter.

Badger stood there, furious. He'd only sent the damn cheque because the penguin was called Peerless. He'd expected some recognisable identity. He felt like stomping away in disgust. Then he saw that one of the penguins was lying apart from all the others, immersed in the water, where it lapped against the nettles. He stared at this one. It lay in the pond like a human being might lie in a bed, with the water covering its chest.

'There he is," said Kevin suddenly. "That's Peerless."

Badger walked nearer. Peerless stood up and looked at him. A weak sun came out and shone on the dark head of Peerless and on the nettles, springy and green.

"All right," said Badger. "Like to stay here a while by myself, if that's OK with you."

"Sure," said Kevin. "Just don't give them any food, will you? It could be harmful."

Kevin walked away over the meadow where the donkeys wandered and Badger stayed very still, watching Peerless. The other penguins queued, like children, for a turn on the plastic slide, but Peerless showed no interest in it at all. He just stayed where he was, on the edge of the pond, going in and out, in and out of the dank water. It was as though he constantly expected something consoling from the water and then found that it wasn't there, but yet expected it again, and then again discovered its absence. And Badger decided, after a while, that he understood exactly what was wrong: the water was too warm. This penguin longed for an icy sea.

Badger sat down on the grass. He didn't care that it was damp. He closed his eyes.

★

It's the beginning of the school term and Badger is unpacking his trunk. He's fourteen years old. He lays his red-and-brown rug on his iron bed in the cold dormitory. Other boys are making darts out of paper and chucking them from bed to bed. Peerless's name is not on the dormitory list.

The Ogre appears at the door and the dart-throwing stops. Boys stand to attention, like army cadets. The Ogre comes over to Badger and puts a hand on his shoulder, and the hand isn't heavy as it usually is, but tender, like the hand of a kind uncle.

"Newbold," he says. "Come up to my study."

He follows the Ogre up the polished main stairs, stairs upon which the boys are not normally allowed to tread. He can smell the sickly wood polish, smell the stale pipe smoke in the Ogre's tweed clothes.

He's invited to sit down in the Ogre's study, on an old red armchair. And the Ogre's eyes watch him nervously. Then the Ogre says: "It concerns Peerless. As his friend, you have the right to know. His mother died. I'm afraid that Peerless will not be returning to the school."

Badger looks away from the Ogre, out at the autumn day; at the clouds carefree and white, at the chestnut leaves flying around in the wind.

"I see," he manages to say. And he wants to get up, then, get out of this horrible chair and go away from here, go to where the leaves are falling. But something in the Ogre's face warns him not to move. The Ogre is struggling to tell him something else and is pleading for time in which to tell it. I may be "the Ogre", says the terrified look on his face, but I'm also a man.

"The thing is…" he begins. "The thing is, Newbold, Peerless was very fond of his mother. You see?"

"See what, sir?"

"Well. He found it impossible. Her absence. As you know, he was a dreaming kind of boy. He was unable to put up any resistance to grief."

★

That evening, Verity made a lamb stew. It was fragrant with rosemary and served with mashed potato and fresh kale. Badger opened a bottle of red wine.

Verity was quiet, yet attentive to him, waiting for him to speak to her. But for a long time Badger didn't feel like speaking. He just felt like eating the good stew and sipping the lovely wine and listening to the birds fall silent in the garden and the ancient electric clock ticking on the kitchen wall.

Eventually, Verity said: "When I said what I said about you letting people go hang, Badger, I was being horribly thoughtless. For a moment I'd completely forgotten about Anthony Peerless."

Badger took another full sip of the wine, then he said: "It's all right, darling. No offence. How were the Battered Wives?"

"OK. Now, I want you to tell me about the penguins. Are they being properly looked after?"

He knew she was humouring him, that she didn't care one way or the other whether a bunch of penguins lived or died. But the wine was making him cheerful, almost optimistic, so he chose to say to her: "The place is nice. But the penguin pool's not cold enough. In the summer, they could die."

"That's a shame."

"I won't let it happen. I've got a plan."

"Tell me?" said Verity

She poured him some more wine. The stew was back in the oven, keeping warm. Mozart was softly playing next door. This was how home was meant to be.

"Ice," said Badger. "I'm going to keep them supplied with ice."

He saw Verity fight against laughter. Her mouth opened and closed—that scarlet mouth he used to adore. Then she smiled kindly. "Where will you get that amount of ice from?"

"The sea," he said. "I'll buy it from the trawlermen."

"Oh," she said. "Good idea, Badger."

"It'll be time-consuming, fetching it, lugging it over to the Sanctuary, but I don't mind. It'll give me something to do."

"Yes, it will."

"And Peerless…"

"What?"

"He seems to suffer the most with things as they are. But the ice should fix it."

"Good," said Verity. "Very good."

★

He lined the boot of his car with waterproof sheets. He bought a grappling hook for handling the ice blocks. He christened it "the Broderick". Despite the sheeting, Badger's car began to smell of the sea. He knew the fisherman thought he was a crazy old party.

But at the pond, now, when the penguins saw him coming, lugging the ice on an ancient luge he'd found in the garage, they came waddling to him and clustered round him as he slowly lifted the end of the luge and let the ice slide into the water. Then they dived in and climbed up on to the ice, or swam beside it, rubbing their heads against it. And he thought, as he watched them, that this was the thing he'd been waiting for, to alter the lot of someone or something. All he'd done was to change the water temperature of a pond in the middle of a Suffolk field by a few degrees. As world events went, it was a pitiful contribution, but he didn't care. Badger Newbold wasn't the kind of man who had ever been able to change the world, but at least he had changed this. Peerless the penguin was consoled by the cool water. And now, when Verity asked him what he was going to do on any particular morning, Badger would be able to reply that he was going to do the ice.

★

From this time on, in Badger's nightmares, the death of Anthony Peerless was a different one…

Peerless has come to stay with him in Suffolk. There are midnight feasts and whispered conversations in the dark.

Then, one morning, Peerless goes out alone on his bicycle. He rides to the dunes and throws his bicycle down on to the soft sand. He walks through the marram grass down to the sea, wearing corduroy trousers and an old brown sweater and a familiar jacket, patched and worn. It's still almost summer, but the sea is an icy, meticulous blue. Peerless starts to swim. His face, with its high colour, begins to pale and pale until he's lost in the cold vastness. He floats serenely, silently down. He floats towards a vision of green grass, towards the soft smell of daisies.

> *…overhead - look overhead*
> *Among the blossoms white and red.*

"It's still almost summer, but the sea is an icy, meticulous blue."

Strawberry Jam

When I was fourteen, in 1957, my mother died. We buried her in the village graveyard and I wore new black shoes with high heels at her funeral. Sudden loss and the pinch of fashionable shoes were then and ever afterwards connected in my mind. I still feel my own mortality most acutely in my feet.

It was winter. My father studied recipes for hot puddings. "Staying alive means keeping warm," he said. Suet and sponge were it, our existence. Yet I was growing, getting tall and thin, and these limbs of mine were as cold as marble. I put the high-heeled shoes away, wrapped up in tissue paper. When I remembered my mother, I thought about my own vanity and wondered when my life would begin. Passion, I believed, might warm me up. Folded inside one of my bedsocks was a photograph of Alan Ladd.

As the spring came and the evenings got lighter, I spent a lot of time looking out of my window, as if trying to see in the familiar landscape of our neighbours' garden the arrival of the future. This garden, separated from ours by only a picket fence, was never dug, pruned or tended in any way and in summer puffs of seed streamed off into the wind from its thistles and willow-herb and tall grasses, sowing themselves in our lawn and in my mother's rockery. She had been a polite and timid person. Only once had she plucked up her courage and knocked on our neighbours' back door and announced with great grief in her voice: "Your weeds are making my task very difficult, Mr Zimmerli."

Walter Zimmerli had come out and stared at his wilderness, sizing it up like a man at a heifer auction.

"The weeds?"

"Yes. They re-seed themselves all over the place."

"And the solution?"

"Well, if you could root them out…"

"But look how splendid is the pink colour!"

"I know…"

"We like this: nature not disturbed. This is important to Jani, I'm afraid."

The only trees in the Zimmerlis' garden were fruit trees: an old and graceful Victoria Plum, a crab apple and some lichen-covered Bramleys. Every Christmas, Walter Zimmerli set up a ladder and gathered the mistletoe that sprouted near the tops of the Bramleys. In summer, out came the ladder again and the crab apples and plums were picked, but most of the Bramleys left to the wasps and the autumn gales. We didn't know why at first, till Jani Zimmerli came round with a jar of crab apple jelly for us. My mother tried to thank her. "It is not thanks," said Jani, "Walter and I, we love jam."

So in April I watched the blossom creeping out on the Zimmerlis' trees and spots creeping out on my face. The sweet puddings steamed in my blood. My father began to learn the recipes by heart.

Then, Mrs Lund arrived.

I saw her first from my window. Walter and Jani Zimmerli came out into their orchard. It was dusk. Mrs Lund followed them like a little shadow. The three stood together quietly and stared at the trees. Mrs Lund set down the suitcase she was carrying and Walter turned to her and said something in German. Mrs Lund nodded and Jani nodded and then they picked up the suitcase and went back inside the house. At supper, I told my father: "The Zimmerlis have got a friend staying."

"Are you sure?"

"Yes. I saw her. She's quite old."

My father put down his knife and fork on a plate of dumplings and gravy he couldn't eat. "I suppose you'll be keeping watch," he said.

Watching the Zimmerlis had been an occupation of mine since the first summer of their arrival, but I used to watch the front of their house—from a window seat in our sitting room. I would wrap my face in the lace curtains and stare out at them. "Holly!" my mother would snap. "Leave them alone!" But I couldn't leave them alone because I was fascinated by what they were doing. Outside their door, on the grass verge, they'd set up a table, shaded on hot days by a large faded umbrella, and here they sat—sometimes both of them, sometimes Jani alone—hour after hour, waiting for people to pass. They were trying to sell jam. The jam was delicious—we were among the few who knew this—and Jani had made pretty gingham covers for the array of pots. But two things struck me as strange. First of all, our houses are on a narrow, out-of-the-way road down which almost no one travels, so that Jani and Walter could sit at their little stall for an entire afternoon without selling one single jar of jam. Secondly, whenever a car did stop, the Zimmerlis never seemed to be content with the small commercial transaction, but began to treat the customers like old friends, talking and laughing and invariably trying to persuade them to go into their house for a glass of sherry.

My mother didn't approve of my spying on the Zimmerlis. When I told her they invited strangers in, she didn't believe me. "The Zimmerlis wouldn't do that," she said, "they keep themselves to themselves." She died disbelieving me. She'd never heard them pleading with strangers, "Just to keep a little company," but I had. And I also knew something else: the jam customers were the only people who ever went into that house. No real friends ever arrived. We, their closest neighbours, were never invited past the kitchen door. They gave us jam. They said good evening from their perch up the ladders. But that was all. No car except theirs ever stood in the drive. Even at Christmas their house was silent and the door closed.

No light ever went on in the guest room. It was as if they had no past and courted no future, only this fleeting present—a few coins in the money tin and the company of strangers.

Now, this elderly woman had arrived. For the first time ever, a light went on in the Zimmerlis' spare room and I saw Jani at the window, drawing the curtains. I imagined this shadowy person, covered with the fat Austrian feather quilt, her possessions folded and put away. I imagined Jani and Walter next door to her, talking in whispers.

And then I learned her name. I was in our garden, putting new alpines in my mother's rockery. I looked up and saw someone standing at the picket fence and it was her. I smiled.

"Very good weather," she said.

"Yes. The winter's over, probably."

"I think you must be Holly?"

"Yes."

"Well. Jani and Walter have spoken of you."

"Have they?"

"Oh yes."

I stood up. I thought about my face wrapped in the lace curtains, a gross, gawping bride. Since my mother's death, I suffered very often from shame.

"My name is Mrs Lund," said the woman.

"How do you do?" I said.

★

The weather people told us a hot summer was coming. The weeds in the Zimmerlis' patch were growing green again through last year's fallen mass. I waited for the Zimmerlis to set up the jam stall, but it didn't appear. They had company now, they had Mrs Lund. I imagined them drinking sherry with her and talking about Viennese teashops full of delicate confectionary—apricot tartlets, apple flan, damson shortcake. She was their past, come to sweeten them, and for a time I envied them, because I knew my own past—our warm, comfortable life with my mother—could only come back as a cold memory. But after a few weeks of Mrs Lund's visit, I began to notice a change in the Zimmerlis: they were losing weight.

I had never known how old they were. Walter seemed older (fatter, with wilder greying hair) than my father, who was forty-three, and Jani seemed younger (more buxom, dimpled and healthy) than my mother, who had been forty-one. Certainly, I'd always thought of them as large, not bony and big as I was, but wide and squashy as only people nearing middle age become. But now they seemed reduced. Walter's belly was smaller; Jani's arms, hanging up her napkins and her tablecloths, were thinner. Even Walter's laugh, not often heard these days, seemed altered, no longer the laugh of a heavy man.

The diminution of the Zimmerlis struck me as odd. Then, one night very late (I'd taken Alan Ladd out of my bedsock and was smoothing him out on my dressing table) I heard Jani weeping. I turned my light off and went to the window. Jani was sitting on her terrace and her face was buried in her lap. After a while, Walter came out and knelt down beside her and leant his head against her shoulder. He spoke to her very softly and this was the first time that I ever thought of the German language as a comforting thing. But I also had a strong feeling— confirmed by my own sleeplessness—that something important was about to happen. That same night, Mrs Lund disappeared.

I woke very late the next morning. It was Saturday. An unfamiliar *chock, chock* sound had woken me. When I looked out, I saw what it was: Walter Zimmerli was digging his garden! I called my father and we watched him together. A large patch of weeds had already been cleared and Walter's back was soaked with sweat. He worked on without stopping, thrusting the spade into the earth, levering with his foot, smashing the clods as he turned them over.

"Why?" I whispered.

"'Bout time, anyway," said my father.

"Yes, but why? Why now?"

"Dunno, Holly. People are often a mystery. You'll find that out."

My father went downstairs and I stayed at the window. Then my father returned with hot muffins and milky coffee on a tray. He said I needed spoiling. Grief, he said, is very tiring. He made me get back into bed to eat the breakfast. Then I dozed. I was tired. And I had a dream that Walter Zimmerli had killed Mrs Lund, smashed her on the back of the neck with a marble rolling pin, and buried her in the garden. That was why—yes, of course, that was why—Jani had wept. They had murdered Mrs Lund.

Then it was mid-day and I was at the window again. On and on Walter worked, with the spring sunshine hot on his neck. Nearly half of his garden had been cleared when I heard Jani call him in. He left his spade sticking into the earth.

His subterfuge isn't bad, I thought. If he'd cleared only a very small patch, a patch only three or four times larger, say, than the spot where Mrs Lund is buried, this might have appeared odd. As it is, he pretends he's weeding his whole garden, getting rid of the willow-herb at last, answering his neighbours' complaints. But he hasn't fooled me! I saw Mrs Lund die in my dream. I saw Walter go out and begin to dig in the dead of morning. I saw Jani trying to help him, pulling with all her might at the grasses. Then I saw them go inside and wrap Mrs Lund's body in a faded rug and stagger out, one holding her shoulders, one her feet, and lay her in a shallow trough that was only just deep enough to hide her. They smashed her in. Hurriedly, Walter piled the earth on top of her and began—even though he was tired by this time and aching with fear—to turn the soil around and beyond the grave. And this is when I began to hear it, the *chock, chock* of his terrible digging…

I don't remember what we did that weekend. I know my father took me somewhere, to see my cousins perhaps, who lived in a big house by a river. All I know is that Walter Zimmerli worked on and on, almost without pausing until, by dusk on Sunday, no trace of the grass or thistle or willow-herb remained and the earth was raked flat like a seed bed and in the twilight Jani made a bonfire of the weeds and I heard the Zimmerlis laughing.

During the next week, they began to plant. On their back porch were piles of wooden boxes stacked up. Each box contained twenty or thirty straggly plants and they set them in rows measured out with string about three feet apart. And I knew what they were: strawberries. I wanted to say to my father, "They're planting strawberries on Mrs Lund!" But I didn't. I just stood on our side of the picket fence and stared at the Zimmerlis crouched down and at Jani's skirt in the mud, and then I offered to help. They stood up and smiled at me. "Ah," said Walter, "very fortunate, eh Jani? Holly can be in charge of the straw."

As I worked, moving down the lines very slowly with the sacks of straw, I tried to test the feel of the earth under my boots. I knew where the body was—roughly—but the soil in the right hand corner of the garden was as flat and even as the rest. They did a good job, I thought. No one will ever know. Except me. Unless, of course, someone comes over from Vienna and they start to search. And I imagined how it would be then: they would find traces of Mrs Lund's visit in the house—tweed skirts, shoes of Swiss leather, a tortoiseshell hairbrush bundled out of sight in a wardrobe—and then of course they would begin to dig…

We finished planting the strawberries the following weekend. My father said I looked pink from all the fresh air and work, and I did find that my skinny hands and feet had been warmed up. Alan Ladd in my bedsock felt snug. And then the strangest, most unexpected thing happened: Walter Zimmerli gave me a key to his house. "We have to go away, Holly," he said. "We have to go back to Vienna to sort out some papers and things and we would be so grateful if you might water our many house plants."

"Yes," said Jani "we would be grateful. But we ask you not to touch anything, any precious things, and let no one else come in. We trust you to be this little caretaker."

I looked at the Zimmerlis: two solemn faces; two bodies, once weighty, growing thin with anxiety and guilt. "Of course," I said. "I'd be happy to take care of your plants. And if the weather's very dry, I'll put our sprinkler on the strawberries."

★

It was May. For my birthday, my father bought me a blue and white polka-dot skirt and a white webbing belt. He said I was getting to look like Debbie Reynolds. "My hair's thin," I said, "perhaps it's our diet." So he started to learn a new set of recipes, casseroles and hotpots and fruit fools, and we began to flourish.

Crime detection, wrote the Chief Constable of the Suffolk police in our church news sheet, *requires faith, hope, intelligence and also physical courage.* I cut these words out and hid them in a shell box my mother had given me. The Zimmerlis left very early one morning and all the blinds and shutters in the house were closed.

"I have a feeling," I said to my father, "that they'll never come back."

"Why do you think that?"

"I don't know," I said dreamily, "I have these peculiar thoughts."

I made myself wait one week before going into the Zimmerlis' house. I ate well and went for long rides on my bicycle to make myself strong. Then I chose a Sunday morning. My father had gone to the pub. I took a watering-can and the door key and a wire coat-hanger. When I opened the Zimmerlis' back door, all I could see was darkness.

I was looking for two things: the murder weapon and the locked wardrobe. I flicked a light switch in the hall, but no light came on. The electricity had been turned off. I made my way in the dark kitchen. I set down the watering-can. Slowly, I tipped the slats of the Venetian blinds and sunlight fell in stripes on to the scrubbed table and an ornate dresser painted red and green. I opened every door and found all kinds of utensil—whisks and strainers, graters and slicers and scoops—but no rolling pin. *The murder weapon,* said the voice of the Chief Constable, *is seldom easily found. However, it is sometimes possible to infer guilt precisely from the absence of the instrument of death from its accustomed place.*

I stood and looked at the room where Jani Zimmerli had made her cauldrons of jam. Was it possible that this Austrian woman with her sweet tooth never made pastry? Never made flans or strudel or pies? I didn't think so. I imagined Walter and Jani—at least until they began to get thin—living on this kind of food, and yet nowhere in the kitchen could I find a rolling pin.

There were some fleshy plants on the window sill. I ran water into my can and doused them, pondering what to do next. No doubt my search for the rolling pin was futile. It lay, I imagined, in the mud of the river that flowed past my cousins' house. When the summer holidays came, I would announce a diving competition. Meanwhile, I had to find the locked wardrobe.

I made my way upstairs, carrying the wire hanger. I knew which side of the house the guest room was on, but I decided, first, to go into the Zimmerlis' own bedroom. Drawing the heavy curtains, I noticed that the room had a strange smell. The odour in this one room was warm and spicy, as if Jani and Walter had been in it only moments before. I looked at the bed, covered with a heavy, intricate patchwork quilt, and at Jani's little dressing-table mirror draped with scarves and amber beads and a sudden, unexpected feeling of sadness came to me. It was obvious—so obvious!—that Jani and Walter had been happy here, in this room, in this house, but now, because of what they had done, their happiness was over and they would never be able to come back here. Change had come. To them. To me. Mrs Lund lay under the strawberries; my mother lay under the churchyard turf. One part of my life was gone.

I sat down on the Zimmerlis' bed. I didn't cry. I made myself think about Alan Ladd and French kissing and the future. I promised myself I would take my black high heels out of the tissue paper and try them on.

I got up and smoothed the quilt and walked, upright and purposeful, to the room where Mrs Lund had slept. I lifted the blind and looked around. There were two beds in the room, both narrow. Between them was an old washstand with a flowery jug and bowl. On the wood floor was a faded rug resembling almost perfectly the rug I'd seen in my dream. In the corner of the room, behind the door, was a mahogany wardrobe. This was so exactly like the wardrobe I'd imagined (mirror glass on the front, ornate classical carvings along the top) that I caught my breath and now hardly dared to move towards it. I looked down at the wire coat-hanger in my hand. In stories, people opened doors with coat-hangers, but would I be able to do it? I stepped forward. Only then did I notice that the key of the wardrobe was there in the lock.

Over the years, I've thought about it very many times, that moment of opening the wardrobe in Mrs Lund's room. I see myself exactly as I was then, reflected in the mirror, wearing my blue polka-dot skirt, my face solemn but full of expectation, on the brink of a momentous discovery. And then I see inside of the wardrobe, not, as I had imagined, filled with Mrs Lund's possessions, but completely empty except for one small object, a black leatherbound notebook. These things made a kind of tableau, like a snapshot. I caught it then and I have it still in my mind, a split second of the future, waiting.

I picked up the notebook, sat down on one of the beds and opened it. On the first page, in fine italic handwriting, were the words: *Tagebuch von J.B. Zimmerli*—the diary of J.B. Zimmerli. Above the first entry were written the date and place: *Wien, November 1937*. I turned the pages, understanding hardly a word of the careful handwriting, but noting dates and places. The entries ceased, with several blank pages remaining, in March 1938. As I came to the final entry, something fell out of the notebook on to the floor. I picked it up. It was a photograph of two children, a boy and a girl, aged perhaps ten and eight respectively. It was summer in the picture. The two children squinted into bright light. Behind them was the glimpse of a lake.

★

That night, I tried to sort it all out in my head. I'd found nothing in the Zimmerlis' house, apart from the absence of the rolling pin, that proved them guilty of Mrs Lund's murder. No possessions stowed away, no sign of her suitcase. I'd gone into every room. I'd tried to think clearly, like a proper detective, aware that clues are not always hidden, but sometimes in plain view, but the longer I searched, the more I began to doubt my first conclusion. It was possible, after all, that Mrs Lund had left very late on the night that I saw Jani crying. A taxi could have come for her, or Walter could have driven her to the station. Perhaps, even, she had left *before* Jani's weeping and it was precisely because Mrs Lund had left that Jani was so upset? And what about the digging? Well, here too, there were logical explanations: Walter's neighbours, including my mother, had been nagging him to do something about his weeds for long enough. Perhaps Mrs Lund, too, had ticked him off and even given him the idea of planting the strawberries.

I decided I would let the whole matter rest for a while. Already my brain felt tired with it and I was beginning to feel glad that I didn't work for the Suffolk Constabulary. I would go in from time to time and water the house plants and I would make sure the strawberries didn't die. And I would wait. In time, I thought, I will probably understand.

The only thing I'd taken from the house was the photograph of the children. I looked at it for a long time and the longer I looked, the more I became convinced that these were the children of Walter and Jani. Because it had always seemed strange to me that the Zimmerlis, who appeared so contented with each other, hadn't got their own family. Had something terrible happened to these children? Was it for them that Jani cried? Were the strangers, clutching their pots of jam, the only people to be told of the tragedy? Was this their *function*, to be silent, anonymous listeners? My father often said he found it easier to talk about my mother's death to strangers than to his friends. One day, he said, he told the lift-man at his office and the lift-man had been very nice to him. If this was true for my father, perhaps it was true for Walter and Jani?

As the days passed, I found I was getting very fond of the photograph. I could imagine the scenery behind the children: the huge lake, a hazy shore line, incredible mountains with snow on their peaks. It calmed me to think of a foreign place—as if part of the future might take place in it. I hid the photograph in my other bedsock, but the nights were warmer now, so the socks and the pictures lay folded under my pillow.

★

As the weathermen had predicted, that summer of 1957 was very hot. Through the first two weeks of June, my father and I watered the Zimmerlis' strawberries and by the third week the strawberries were ripe. There was no sign of Walter and Jani and the birds had already begun to peck at the fruit. We stood by our fence and surveyed the crop.

"Terrible waste," said my father.

"Let's pick them," I said "and make jam."

We bought a preserving pan. In our larder, we found dozens of jam jars, brown with dust, saved by my mother for this day she would never see. On the evening the jam was labeled and put back into the larder— thirteen pounds of it in twenty-one jars—Walter and Jani returned. We saw them kneeling down in the strawberry beds and lifting the leaves to search for the fruit. I called from my upstairs window: "Don't worry! It's all safe!" And when I took the jam round to them the next day, their gratitude seemed to overflow, as if I'd brought them something of great value.

"So kind, Walter, isn't it?" said Jani, picking up one of the pots. "So much work and kindness."

"Indeed," said Walter, "indeed this is most thoughtful."

"You could sell it on the road," I suggested.

"Yes,' said Jani, 'but you must have all the money. Holly must have the profit."

"Yes,' said Walter, "and next year too. The plants will grow a little larger and we shall have a better crop."

"It's kind of you," I said, "but you don't have to give me any money."

"It was as if they had no past and courted no future, only this fleeting present-"

"But we want to do this," said Jani, "maybe you can buy a polka blouse to match your skirt."

I returned the house key to them. As I went to the door, Jani came with me and put her arm, which was still much thinner than it had once been, round my shoulders. "Like you," she said, "we have had some sad times. We lost Walter's mother."

"She died?"

"Yes. In one way so sad, yet in one way happy. Walter's father was killed by the Nazis in 1938 and, since this time, his mother was all these years in an institution, not knowing really what the days were, but thinking the time is before the war and she is a girl again, like you. In her last days, she says to the nurse, do my breasts grow?"

"I'm very sorry," I said.

"Yes," said Jani, "sorrow for all. But that is why we put in the strawberries: *Mutti's* favourite fruit."

I pieced it together then. Mrs Lund—an old friend of the family?— had been a courier. She'd brought not only the news of the death of Walter's mother, but had come to hand over the few possessions of the dead woman, the most important of which was the diary belonging to her husband, J.B. Zimmerli. It was for Walter's mother that Jani had wept, and it was their mourning that had made them thin. There was no body in the garden. The only bit of the mystery I couldn't solve was the identity of the children and I thought now that I never would.

I knew I had to find a way to return the photograph to the wardrobe in Mrs Lund's room, and I had a plan. I would offer to help the Zimmerlis with their jam stall. On a hot afternoon, I would ask them if I could go into the kitchen for a glass of water—a request they couldn't refuse. Then, quickly and silently, I would go upstairs and return the photograph to the black notebook.

But I wanted to have one last look at it. I went up to my room and reached under my pillow to pull out my bedsocks, but they weren't there. With feelings of guilt and dread, I began to search my cupboards and drawers. Alan Ladd I could replace, but those children by the lake, that picture was perhaps all that remained of them. I looked out at the Zimmerlis' house. They'd trusted me, called me their "caretaker" and I'd betrayed them.

And then I saw my bedsocks. They were hanging on the washing line. I ran down to the garden, past my father who was sitting in the sun. I unpegged the socks, which were still damp. "Need them," I said to my father and fled back up to my room.

I put my hand into each of them in turn. Alan Ladd, made of inferior paper, was scrunched into a ball no bigger than a marble. I threw him into my waste paper basket. But the photograph of the children had survived. It was only slightly creased and not faded at all.

I held it against my face, smoothing it out. And then I noticed that there was something different about it. Before the washing, the photograph had been backed with thick, black paper, as if it had been stuck into an album and cut out with part of the album page still glued to it. Now, the black layer of paper wasn't there. I turned the photograph over. In the bottom right hand corner of it, a faded caption was still just decipherable. Dated 1926, it read: *Walter und Jani an der See.* And I understood.

★

For four years, I kept the Zimmerlis' secret. In precisely the way I had planned, I returned the photograph to the notebook and of course Jani and Walter never mentioned either the diary or the picture to me. I grew fond of them and they seemed to become fond of me, yet on certain days, for no reason at all, they would behave very coldly towards me, as if they were saying to me, "Don't come too close. Friendship is too knowing. We prefer still, as always, to talk to strangers, who will never find out anything and who will never come back."

And so, hurt one day by a rebuff of Jani's—"Holly, go home now. You talk too much, always of boyfriends, always of your future. It's boring, you know."—I decided to tell my father. We were sitting together in the kitchen. It was 1961. My father had encouraged his thinning hair to grow long over his ears. I took a sip of the white wine we were drinking and looked at my loving, would-be hippy dad and said solemnly: "Walter and Jani Zimmerli are brother and sister."

He smiled and nodded. "Don't tell the vicar," he said.

The morning I left home for my first term at university, I knocked on the Zimmerlis' back door to say goodbye. Jani opened it, her hands and arms covered in flour. "I'm making pastry," she said, "come in."

We went into her kitchen. I put the kettle on and watched her work. Her arms were fleshy again by this time. When the dough was kneaded to her satisfaction, she began to roll it out, using a painted metal cannister as a rolling pin. It reminded me of a thing my mother used to do: when she planted beans, she'd tread in the soil with her boot and roll it flat with an old tin barrel.

A Shooting Season

"You're writing a *what*?"

"A novel."

Looking away from him, nervously touching her hair, Anna remembered, the last time I saw him my hair wasn't grey.

"Why the hell are you writing a novel?"

Grey hairs had sprouted at forty-one. Now, at forty-five, she sometimes thought, my scalp is exhausted, that's all, like poor soil.

"I've wanted to write a novel ever since I was thirty. Long before, even ..."

"You never told me."

"No. Of course not."

"Why 'Of course not'?"

"You would have laughed, as you're laughing now."

Anna had always been enchanted by his laugh. It was a boy's giggle; (you climbed a cold dormitory stairway and heard it bubble and burst behind a drab door!) yet their son didn't have it: at sixteen, he had the laugh of a rowdy man.

"I don't approve."

"No."

"It's an act of postponed jealousy."

Well, if so, then long postponed. Six years since their separation; four since the divorce and his remarriage to Susan, the pert blonde girl who typed his poems. And it wasn't jealousy surely? In learning to live without him, she had taught herself to forget him utterly. If she heard him talk on the radio, she found herself thinking, his cadences are echoing Dylan Thomas these days; he's remembered how useful it is, if you happen to be a poet, also to be Welsh. Three years older than her, he had come to resemble a Welsh hillside—craggy outcrop of a man, unbuttoned to weather and fortune, hair wiry as gorse. Marcus. Fame clung to his untidy look. No doubt, she thought, he's as unfaithful to Susan as he was to me.

"How did it start?"

The novel-writing, he meant, but he had a way, still, of sending fine ripples through the water of ordinary questions which invited her to admit: I was in love with him for such a long time that parting from him was like drowning. When I was washed ashore, the sediment of him still clogged me.

"I found there were things I wanted to say."

"Oh, there always were!"

"Yes, but stronger now. Before I get old and start forgetting."

"But a *novel*?"

"Why not?"

"You were never ambitious."

No. Not when she was his: Mrs Marcus Ridley, wife of the poet. Not while she bore his children and made rugs while he wrote and they slept.

"Do your pockets still have bits of sand in them?"

He laughed, took her strong wrist and held her hand to his face. "I don't know. No one empties them for me."

★

Anna had been at the rented cottage for three weeks. A sluggish river flowed a few yards from it: mallard and moorhen were the companions of her silence, the light of early morning silver. In this temporary isolation, she had moved contentedly in her summer sandals, setting up a work table in the sunshine, another indoors by the fire. Her novel crept to a beginning, then began to flow quietly like the river. She celebrated each day's work with two glasses, sometimes more, of the home-made wine she had remembered to bring with her. She slept well with the window wide open on the Norfolk sky. She dreamed of her book finished and bound. Then one morning Margaret, her partner in her craft business, telephoned. The sound of the telephone ringing was so unfamiliar that it frightened her. She remembered her children left on their own in London; she raced to answer the unforeseen but now obvious emergency. But no, said Margaret, no emergency, only Marcus.

"Marcus?"

"Yes. Drunk and full of his songs. Said he needed to see you."

"And you told him where I was?"

"Yes. He said if I didn't, he'd pee on the pottery shelf."

★

"Marcus."

The rough feel of his face was very familiar; she might have touched it yesterday. She thought suddenly, for all his puerile needs, he's a man of absolute mystery; I never understood him. Yet they had been together ten years. The Decade of the Poet she called it, wanting to bury him with formality and distance. And yet he surfaced in her: she seldom read a book without wondering, how would Marcus have judged that? And then feeling irritated by the question. On such occasions, she would always remind herself: he doesn't even bother to see the children, let alone me. He's got a new family (Evan 4, Lucy 3) and they, now, take all his love—the little there ever was in him to give.

"You look so healthy, Anna. Healthy and strong. I suppose you always were strong."

"Big-boned, my mother called it."

"How is your mother?"

"Dead."

"You never let me know."

"No. There was no point."

"I could have come with you—to the funeral or whatever."

"Oh, Marcus..."

"Funerals are ghastly. I could have helped you through."

"Why don't you see the children?"

He let her hand drop. He turned to the window, wide open on the now familiar prospect of reed and river. Anna noticed that the faded corduroy jacket he was wearing was stretched tight over his back. He seemed to have outgrown it.

"Marcus...?"

He turned back to her, hands in his pockets.

"No accusations. No bloody accusations!"

Oh yes, she noticed, there's the pattern: I ask a question, Marcus says it's inadmissible, I feel guilty and ashamed...

"It's a perfectly reasonable question."

"Reasonable? It's a guilt-inducing, jealous, mean-minded question. You know perfectly well why I don't see the children: because I have two newer, younger and infinitely more affectionate children, and these newer, younger and infinitely more affectionate children are bitterly resented by the aforementioned older, infinitely less affectionate children. And because I am a coward."

He should be hit, she thought, then noticed that she was smiling.

"I brought some of my home-made wine," she said, "it's a disgusting looking yellow, but it tastes rather good. Shall we have some?"

"Home-made wine? I thought you were a business*person*. When the hell do you get time to make wine?"

"Oh Marcus, I have plenty of time."

Anna went to the cold, pamment-floored little room she had decided to think of as "the pantry". Its shelves were absolutely deserted except for five empty Nescafé jars, a dusty goldfish bowl (the debris of another family's Norfolk summer) and her own bottles of wine. It was thirty-five years since she had lived in a house large enough to have a pantry, but now, in this cupboard of a place, she could summon memories of

Hodgson, her grandfather's butler, uncorking Stones ginger beer for her and her brother on timeless summer evenings—the most exquisite moments of all the summer holidays. Then, one summer, she found herself there alone. Hodgson had left. Her brother Charles had been killed at school by a cricket ball.

Anna opened a bottle of wine and took it and two glasses out to her table in the garden, where Marcus had installed himself. He was looking critically at her typewriter and at the unfinished pages of her book lying beside it.

"You don't mean to say you're typing it?"

She put the wine and the glasses on the table. She noticed that the heavy flint she used as a paperweight had been moved.

"Please don't let the pages blow away, Marcus."

"I'm sure it's a mistake to type thoughts directly on to paper. Writing words by hand is part of the process."

"Your process."

"I don't know any writers who type directly."

"You know me. Please put the stone back, Marcus."

He replaced the pages he had taken up, put the flint down gently and spread his wide hand over it. He was looking at her face.

"Don't write about me, Anna, will you?"

She poured the wine. The sun touched her neck and she remembered its warmth with pleasure.

"Don't make me the villain."

She handed him his glass of wine. Out in the sunshine, he looked pale beside her. A miraculous three weeks of fine weather had tanned her face, neck and arms, whereas he... how did he spend his days now? She didn't know. He looked as if he'd been locked up. Yet he lived in the country with his new brood. She it was—and their children—who had stayed on in the London flat.

"How's Susan?"

No. She didn't want to ask. Shouldn't have asked. She'd only asked

in order to get it over with: to sweep Susan and his domestic life to the
back of her mind, so that she could let herself be nice to him, let herself
enjoy him.

"Why ask?"

"To get it over with!"

He smiled. She thought she sensed his boyish laughter about to
surface.

"Susan's got a lover."

Oh damn him! Damn Marcus! Feeling hurt, feeling cheated,
he thought I'd be easy consolation. No wonder the novel annoys him;
he sees the ground shifting under him, sees a time when he's not the
adored, successful granite he always thought he was.

"Damn the lover."

"What?"

He'd looked up at her, startled. What he remembered most vividly
about her was her permanence. The splash of bright homespun colour
that was Anna: he had only to turn his head, open a door, to find her
there. No other wife or mistress had been like her; these had often been
absent when he'd searched for them hardest. But Anna had always
wanted to be there.

"I'm not very interested in Susan's lover."

"No. He isn't interesting. He's a chartered surveyor."

"Ah. Well, reliable probably."

"Do you think so? Reliable, are they, as a breed? He looks pitiful
enough to be it. Perhaps that's what she wants."

"And you?"

"Me?"

"What do you want, Marcus? Did you come here just to tell me
your wife had a lover?"

"Accusations again. All the bloody little peeves!"

"I want to know why you came here."

"So do I."

"What?"

"So do I want to know. All I know is that I want to see you. If that's not good enough for you, I'll go away."

Further along the river, she could hear the mallard quacking. Some evenings at sunset, she had walked through the reeds to find them (two pairs, one pair with young) and throw in scraps for them. Standing alone, the willows in front of her in perfect silhouette, she envied the ducks their sociability. No one comes near them, she thought, only me standing still. Yet they have everything—everyone—they need.

"I love it here."

She had wanted to sit down opposite Marcus with her glass of wine, but he had taken the only chair. She squatted, lifting her face to the sun. She knew he was watching her.

"Do you want me to go away?"

She felt the intermittent river breeze on her face, heard the pages of her novel flap under the stone. She examined his question. Knew that it confused her, and set it aside.

"The novel's going to be about Charlie."

"Charlie?"

"My brother Charles. Who died at school. I'm imagining that he lived on, but not as him, as a girl."

"Why as a girl?"

"I thought I would understand him better as a girl."

"Will it work?"

"The novel?"

"Giving Charlie tits?"

"Yes, I think so. It also means she doesn't have to play cricket and risk being killed."

"I'd forgotten Charlie."

"You never knew him."

"I knew him as a boy—through your memories. He of Hodgson's ginger beer larder!"

"Pantry."

She's got stronger, Marcus decided. She's gone grey and it suits her. And she's still wearing her bright colours. Probably makes not just her own clothes now, but ponchos and smocks and bits of batik to sell in her shops. And of course her son's friends fall in love with her. She's perfect for a boy: bony, maternal and sexy. Probably her son's in love with her too.

"Can I stay for dinner?"

Anna put her glass to her lips and drained it. He always, she thought, made requests sound like offers.

★

Anna scrutinised the contents of the small fridge: milk, butter, a bunch of weary radishes, eggs. Alone, she would have made do with the radishes and an omelette, but Marcus had a lion's appetite. His most potent memory of a poetry-reading fortnight in America was ordering steak for breakfast. He had returned looking ruddy, like the meat.

Anna sighed. The novel had been going well that morning. Charlie, renamed Charlotte, was perched high now above her cloistered schooldays on the windswept catwalk of a new university. Little gusts of middle-class guilt had begun to pick at her well-made clothes and at her heart. She was ready for change.

"Charlotte can wait," Marcus told Anna, after her one feeble attempt to send him away. "She'll be there tomorrow and I'll be gone. And anyway, we owe it to each other—one dinner."

I owe nothing, Anna thought. No one (especially not pretty Susan with her tumbling fair hair and her flirtatious eyes) could have given herself—her time, her energy, her love—more completely to one man than she to Marcus. For ten years he had been the landscape that held her whole existence—one scarlet poppy on the hills and crags of him, sharing his sky.

"One dinner!"

★

"But the sun comes up on the strange stretch of river where, only yesterday, they had a life..."

She took the car into Wroxham, bought good dark fillet, two bottles of Beaujolais, new potatoes, a salad and cheese.

While she was gone, he sat at the table in the sunshine, getting accustomed to the gently scented taste of her home-made wine and, despite a promise not to, reading her novel. Her writing bored him after a few pages; he needed her presence, not her thoughts.

I've cried for you, he wanted to tell her. There have been times when—yes, several of them—times when I haven't felt comfortable with the finality of our separation, times when I've thought, there's more yet, I need more. And why couldn't you be part of my life again, on its edge? I would honestly feel troubled less—by Susan's chartered surveyor, by the coming of my forty-ninth birthday—yes, much less, if you were there in your hessian or whatever it is you wear and I could touch you. Because ten years is, after all, a large chunk of our lives, and though I never admit it, I now believe that my best poems were written during those ten and what followed has been mainly repetition. And I wanted to ask you, where are those rugs you made while I worked? Did you chuck them out? Why was the silent making of your rugs so intimately connected to my perfect arrangement of words?

★

"So here we are..."

The evening promised to be so warm that Anna had put a cloth on the table outside and laid it for supper. Marcus had helped her prepare the food and now they sat facing the sunset, watching the colours go first from the river, then from the willows and poplars behind it.

"Remember Yugoslavia?"

"Yes, Marcus."

"Montenegro."

"Yes."

"Those blue thistles."

"Umm."

"Our picnic suppers!"

"Stale bread."

"What?"

"The bread in Yugoslavia always tasted stale."

"We used to make love in a sleeping bag."

"Yes."

Anna thought, it will soon be so dark, I won't be able to see him clearly, just as, in my mind, I have only the most indistinct perception of how he *is* in that hard skin, if I ever knew. For a moment she considered going indoors to get a candle, but decided it would be a waste of time; the breeze would blow it out. And the darkness suits us, suits this odd meeting, she thought. In it, we're insubstantial; we're each imagining the other one, that's all.

"I read the novel, as far as you've gone."

"Yes. I thought you probably would."

"I never pictured you writing."

"No. Well, I never pictured you arriving here. Margaret told me you said you 'needed' me. What on earth did you mean?"

"I think about you—often."

"Since Susan found her surveyor?"

"That's not fair."

"Yes, it's fair. You could have come to see me—and the children—anytime you wanted."

"I wanted..."

"What?"

"Not the children. You."

For a moment Anna allowed herself to remember: "You, in the valley of my arms, /my quaint companion on the mountain./How wisely did I gather you,/my crimson bride..." Then she took a sip of beaujolais and began:

"I've tried."

"What?"

"To love other people. Other men."

"And?"

"The feelings don't seem to last. Or perhaps I've just been unlucky."

"Yes. You deserve someone."

"I don't want anyone, Marcus. This is what I've at last understood. I have the children and the craft shops and one or two men friends to go out with, and now I have the novel..."

"I miss you Anna."

She rested her chin on folded hands and looked at him. Mighty is a perfect word, she thought. To me, he has always seemed mighty. And when he left me, every room, every place I went to was full of empty space. Only recently had I got used to it, decided finally to stop trying to fill it up. And now there he is again, his enormous shadow, darker, nearer than the darkness.

"You see, I'm not a poet anymore."

"Yes, you are, Marcus. I read your new volume..."

"No I'm not. I won't write anything more of value."

"Why?"

"Because I'm floundering, Anna. I don't know what I expect of myself anymore, as a poet or as a man. Susan's destroying me."

"Oh rot! Susan was exactly the woman you dreamed of."

"And now I have dreams of you."

Anna sighed and let Marcus hear the sigh. She got up and walked the few yards to the river and watched it shine at her feet. For the first time that day, the breeze made her shiver.

★

Light came early. Anna woke astonished and afraid. Marcus lay on his stomach, head turned away from her, his right arm resting down the length of her body.

A noise had woken her, she knew, yet there was nothing: only the sleeper's breath next to her and the birds tuning up, like a tiny hidden orchestra, for their full-throated day. Then she heard them: two shots, then a third and a fourth. Marcus turned over, opened his eyes and looked at her. She was sitting up and staring blankly at the open window. The thin curtains moved on a sunless morning.

"Anna..."

The strong hand on her arm wanted to tug her gently down, but she resisted its pressure, stayed still, chin against her knees.

"Someone's shooting."

"Come back to sleep."

"No, I can't. Why would someone be shooting?"

"The whole world's shooting!"

"I must go and see."

Marcus lay still and watched Anna get up. As she pulled on a faded, familiar gown, both had the same thought; it was always like this, Anna getting up first, Marcus in bed half asleep, yet often watching Anna.

"What are you going to do?"

"I don't know. But I have to see."

The morning air was chilly. It was sunless, Anna realised, only because the sun had not yet risen. A mist squatted above the river; the landscape was flattened and obscured in dull white. Anna stared. The dawn has extraordinary purpose, she thought, everything contained, everything shrouded by the light but emerging minute by minute into brightness and shape, so that while I stand still it all changes. She began to walk along the river. The ground under her sandals was damp and the leather soon became slippery. Nothing moved. The familiar breeze had almost died in the darkness, the willow leaves hung limp and wet. Anna stopped, rubbed her eyes.

"Where are you?"

She waited, peering into the mist. The mist was yellowing, sunlight slowly climbing. A dog barked, far off.

"Where are you?"

Senseless question. Where are you? Where are you? Anna walked on. The surface of the water, so near her slippery feet, was absolutely smooth. The sun was climbing fast now and the mist was tumbling, separating, making way for colour and contour. Where *are* you!

The three words came echoing down the years. Anna closed her eyes.

They came and shot the ducks, she told herself calmly. That's all.

Men came with guns and had a duck shoot and the mallard are gone.

When I come down here with my scraps, I won't find them. But that's all. The river flows on. Everything else is just as it was yesterday and the day before and the day before that. I am still Anna. Birds don't matter. I have a book to write. And the sun's coming up...

She was weeping. Clutching her arms inside the sleeves of the faded gown, she walks from room to room in the empty flat. Where are you! London dawn at the grimed net curtains... fruit still in the bowl from which, as he finally went, he stole an orange... nothing changes and yet everything... his smell still on her body... And where am I? Snivelling round the debris of you in all the familiar rooms, touching surfaces you touched, taking an orange from the bowl... Where am I? Weeping. The ducks don't matter. Do they? Keeping hold on what is, on what exists *after* the shot has echoed and gone, this is all that's important, yes, keeping hold on what I have forced myself to become, with all the sanding and polishing of my heart's hardness, keeping hold of my life alone that nothing—surely not the wounds of one night's loving?—can destroy. So just let me wipe my face on the same washed-out corner of a sleeve. And forget. A stranger carries the dead mallard home, dead smeared heads, bound together with twine. But the sun comes up on the same stretch of river where, only yesterday, they had a life...

★

Marcus held Anna. They stood by his car. It was still morning, yet they sensed the tiredness in each other, as if neither had slept at all.

"I'll be going then, old thing. Sorry I was such a miserable bugger. Selfish of me to disturb you with my little problems."

"Oh, you weren't disturbing me."

"Yes, I was. Typical of me: Marcus Ridley's Lament *for* Things as They Are.'

"I don't mind. And last night -"

"Lovely, Anna. Perhaps I'll stop dreaming about you now."

"Yes."

He kissed her cheek and got quickly into the car.

"Good luck with the novel."

"Oh yes. Thank you, Marcus."

"I'll picture you working by your river."

"Come and see the children, Marcus. Please come and see the children."

"Yes. Alright. No promises. Are you going to work on the book today?"

"No, I don't think I can. Not today."

"Poor Anna. I've tired you. Never mind. There's always tomorrow."

"Yes, Marcus," and very gently she reached out and touched his face, "there's always tomorrow."

Wildtrack

Micky Stone, wearing camouflage, crouches in a Suffolk field, shielding his tape recorder from the first falling of snow. It's December. Micky Stone, who is approaching his fiftieth birthday, perfectly remembers touching his mother's fingers as she stood at the metal window of the cottage kitchen, watching snow fall. She was saying something. "Isn't it quiet?" she was saying, but ten year-old Micky was deaf and couldn't hear.

Now, in a field, holding the microphone just above his head, he hears the sounds it gathers: the cawing of rooks, the crackle of beech branches as the birds circle and return. He hears everything perfectly. When he looks down at the tape machine, he hears his head turning inside his anorak hood.

Seven operations there were. Mrs Stone, widowed at thirty-five, sat in the dark of the hospital nights and waited for her son to wake up and hear her say, "it's all right." And after the seventh operation she said, "it's all right now, Micky," and he heard. And sound entered his mind and astonished him. At twelve, he asked his mother: "Who collects the sound of the trains and the sea and the traffic and the birds for the plays on the wireless?" And Mrs Stone, who loved the wireless plays and found in them a small solace in her widowhood, answered truthfully: "I've never thought about it, Micky, but I expect someone goes out with a machine and collects them. I expect a man does." And Micky nodded. "I think I'll become that man," he told her.

It was a job you travelled for. Your life was a scavenge-hunt. You had lists: abattoir, abbey, accordion, balloon ascent, barcarole, beaver and on and on through the alphabet of things living and wild and man-made that breathed or thumped or yodelled or burned or sang. It was a beautiful life, Micky thought. He pitied the millions who sat in rooms all their working days and had never heard a redshank or a bullfrog. Some people said to him, "I bet it's a lonely life, just listening to things, Micky?" But he didn't agree and he thought it presumptuous of people to suggest this. The things he liked listening to least were words.

Yet Micky Stone had a kind of loneliness in him, a small one, growing bigger as he aged. It was connected to the feeling that there had been a better time than now, a short but perfect time, in fact, and that nothing in his life, not even his liking of his work, would ever match it. He remembers this now, as the sky above the field becomes heavy and dark with the snow yet to fall: the time of Harriet Cavanagh, he calls it, or in other words, the heyday.

★

Suffolk is a rich place for sound. Already, in four days, Micky Stone has collected half an hour of different winter birds. His scavenge list includes a working windmill, a town market, a livestock auction and five minutes of sea. He's staying at a bed-and-breakfast in a small town not far from the cottage with the metal windows where he heard his first sounds. He's pleased to be near this place. Though the houses are smarter and the landscape emptier now, the familiar names on the signposts and the big openness of the sky give him a sense of things unaltered. It's not difficult, here, to remember the shy, secretive man he was at nineteen and to recreate in the narrow lanes the awesome sight of Harriet Cavanagh's ramrod back and neat beige bottom sitting on her pony. The thing he loved most about this girl was her deportment. He was a slouch, his mother often told him, a huddler. Harriet Cavanagh was as perfectly straight as a bamboo. And flying like a pennant from her head was her long, straight hair, the colour of cane.

Micky Stone would crouch by the gate at the end of his mother's garden, close his eyes and wait for the first sound of the horse. It always trotted, never walked. Harriet Cavanagh was a person in a hurry, flying into her future. Then, as the clip-clop of the hooves told Micky that the vision was in sight, he'd open his eyes and lift his head and Harriet in her haste would hail him with her riding crop, "Hi, Micky!" and pass on. She'd be out of sight very quickly, but Micky would stand and listen till the sound of the trotting pony had completely died away. When he told his mother that he was going to marry Harriet Cavanagh, she'd sniffed and said unkindly, "Oh yes? And Princess Margaret Rose too, I dare say?" imagining that with these words she'd closed the matter. But the matter of Harriet Cavanagh didn't close. Ever. At fifty, with the winter lying silently about him, Micky Stone knows that it never will. As he packs his microphone away, the snow is falling densely and he hears himself hope that it will smother the fields and block the lanes and wall him up in its whiteness with his fabulous memories.

★

The next morning, as he brushes the snow from the windscreen of his car, he notices that the driver's side window has already been cleared of it—deliberately cleared, he imagines—as if someone had been peering in. Unlocking the door, he looks around at the quiet street of red Edwardian houses with white-painted gables on which the sun is now shining. It's empty of people, but the pavement is patterned with their footprints. They've passed and gone and it seems that one of them stopped and looked into Micky Stone's car.

He loads his equipment and drives out of the town. The roads are treacherous. He's looking forward to hearing the windmill, when, a few miles out of the town, it occurs to Micky that this is one of the stillest days he can remember. Not so much as a breath of wind to turn the sails. He slows it to a stop and winds down the window and listens. The fields and hedgerows are icy, silent, glittering. On a day like this, Harriet Cavanagh once exclaimed as she passed the cottage gate,

"Gosh, it's beautiful, isn't it Micky?" and the bit in the pony's mouth jingled as he sneezed and Micky noticed that the animal's coat was long and wondered if the winter would be hard.

Now he wonders what has become of the exact place by the hawthorn hedge where he used to stand and wait for Harriet on her morning rides. His mother is long dead, but he suspects that the cottage will be there, the windows replaced, perhaps, the boring garden redesigned. So he decides, while waiting for an east wind, to drive to the cottage and ask its owners whether they would mind if he did a wildtrack of their lane.

It's not far. He remembers the way. Through the smart little village of Pensford Green where now, he notices, the line of brick cottages are painted loud, childish colours and only the snow on their roofs unifies them as a rural terrace, then past two fields of apple trees, and there's the lane. What he can't remember now as he approaches it is whether the lane belonged to the house. Certainly, in the time when he lived there no cars ever seemed to come up it, only farmers sometimes and in the autumn the apple pickers and Harriet Cavanagh of course, who seemed, from her lofty seat in the saddle, to own the whole county.

Micky Stone feels nervous as the lane unfolds. The little car slithers. The lane's much longer than he remembers and steeper. The car, lurching up hill, nudges the banks, slews round and stops. Micky restarts the engine, then hears the wheels spin, making deep grooves in the snow. He gets out, looking for something to put under the wheels. The snow's almost knee-deep, and there are no tracks in it except those his car has made. Micky wonders if the present tenants of the cottage sense that they're marooned.

Then it occurs to him that he has the perfect excuse for visiting them: "I took a wrong turning and my car's stuck. I wondered whether you could help me?" Then while they fetch sacks and a shovel from the old black shed, he'll stand waiting by the gate, his feet planted on the exact spot which, thirty years ago, he thought of as hallowed ground.

So he puts on his boots and starts out on foot, deciding not to take his machine. The silence of the morning is astonishing. He passes a holly tree that he remembers. His mother, tall above her slouch-back of a son, used to steal branches from this tree to lay along her Christmas mantelpiece.

The tree wasn't far from the cottage. As he rounds the next bend, Micky expects to see it: the gate, the hawthorn hedge, the graceless little house with its low door. Yet it isn't where he thought it would be. He stops and looks behind him, trying to remember how far they used to walk, carrying the holly boughs. Then he stands still and listens. Often the near presence of a house can be heard: a dog barking, the squeak of a child's swing. But there's nothing at all.

Micky walks on. On his right, soon, he sees a break in the hedge. He hurries the last paces to it and finds himself looking into an empty field. The field slopes away from the hedge, just as the garden used to slope away. Micky walks forward, sensing that there's grass, not plough, under his feet and he knows that the house was here. It never belonged to them, of course. When his mother left, it returned to the farmer from whom she'd rented it for twelve years. She'd heard it was standing empty. It was before the time of the scramble for property. No one had thought of it as a thing of value.

Micky stands for a while where the gate used to be. On my mark, he thinks. Yet the altered landscape behind him robs it of familiarity. It's as if, in removing the house, someone has removed his younger self from the place where he used to stand.

No point in staying, he decides, so he walks slowly back past the holly tree to his car. He gets in, releases the handbrake and lets it slip gently backwards down its own tracks. As the bottom of the lane, he starts the engine, reverses out into the road and drives away.

★

In the afternoon, he goes down to the shingly beach. The sun's low and the wind coming off the sea strong enough to make the sleeves of his anorak flap. He crouches near a breakwater. He sets up his machine, tests for sound levels, then holds the microphone at the ocean. He remembers his instructions: "With the sea recording, Micky, try to get gulls and any other seabirds. And do plenty of selection, strong breakers close-up, smaller splashing waves without much wind, and so on. Use your judgment."

The scene his microphone is gathering is very beautiful. He wishes, for once, that he was gathering pictures as well as sound. The snow still lying high up on the beach and along the sea wall is almost violet-coloured in the descending afternoon. A film maker might wait months to capture this extraordinary light. Micky closes his eyes, forcing himself to concentrate on the sound only. When he opens them again, he sees a man standing still about thirty yards from him and staring at him.

Micky stays motionless, closes his eyes again, hears to his satisfaction gulls calling far off. When he opens his eyes once more, he sees that the man has come nearer, but is standing in the same attitude, intently watching Micky.

So Micky's thoughts return to the morning, to his discovery that someone had been peering into his car, then to his visit to the house which had gone, and he feels, not fear exactly, nor even suspicion, but a kind of troubled excitement and all the questions his mind has been asking for years about this place and the person he loved in it suddenly clamour in him for answers. He looks up at the stranger. He's a tall, straight-standing person. His hands are in the pockets of a long coat. In his stern look and in his straightness, he reminds Micky of Harriet Cavanagh's father, in the presence of whom Micky Stone felt acutely his own lack of height and the rounded disposition of his shoulders. But he tells himself that the fierce Major Cavanagh must now be an old man and this stranger is no more than forty-five, about the age Harriet herself would be.

Micky looks at his watch. He decides he will record three more minutes of sea and that then he will go over to the man and say what he

"Mickey stands for a while where the gate used to be."

now believes he's come here to do: "I'm looking for Harriet Cavanagh. This may sound stupid. Are you in a position to help me?"

Then Micky turns away and tries to concentrate on the waves and the birds. He dreads speaking to the man because he was never any good at expressing himself. When Harriet Cavanagh said of the shiny white morning, "Gosh, it's beautiful!" Micky was struck by her phrase like a whip and was speechless. Harriet had chosen a language that suited her: it was straight and direct and loud. Micky, huddled by his gate, knew that the dumbness of his first ten years had somehow lingered in his brain.

The three minutes seem long. The gulls circle and fight. Micky forces himself not to move a muscle. The sea breaks and is pulled back, rattling the shingle like coins, and breaks again. When Micky at last turns round, the man has gone.

★

On the edge of sleep, Micky hears the wind get up. Tomorrow, he will go to the windmill. He thinks, tonight I can hear my own loneliness inside me, turning.

★

Micky climbs up a broad ladder into the lower section of the mill. Its owner is a narrow-shouldered, rather frail seeming man who seems excited and pleased to show Micky round.

"It's funny," says the skinny man as he opens the trap door to the big working chamber, "my Dad once thought of buying a windmill, but he wanted to chuck out all the machinery and turn the thing into a house. But I'd never do that. I think far too many of the old, useful things have vanished."

Micky nods and they mount a shorter ladder and scramble through the trap into the ancient body of the mill. Light comes from a window below the ratchet wheel and from the pulley hatch, where the sacks of corn are wound up and the bags of milled flour lowered.

"We're only in use for part of the year," says the owner, "but we can lower the grinding wheel so that you can get the sound of it."

Micky nods and walks to the window and looks down. Every few moments his view of the icy fields is slashed by the passing of one of the sails, but he likes the feeling of being high up for once, not crouching or hiding. And as he stares and the arms of the windmill pass and re-pass, he thinks, I must stand up tall now for what I want and what I have always wanted and still do not possess: the sound of Harriet Cavanagh's voice.

"All right, then?" asks the mill owner, disappointed by Micky's silence. "I'll set the wheel, shall I?"

Micky turns, startled. "Thank you," he says. "I'll set up in here. Then I'll do a few minutes outside."

"Good," says the mill owner, then adds, "I like the radio plays. 'The Theatre of the Mind' someone said it was called and I think that's a good description because the mind only needs sound to imagine entire places, entire situations. Isn't that right?"

"Well," says Micky, "yes, I think it is."

★

It's dark by the time Micky gets back to his lodgings. As he goes in, he can smell the meal his landlady is preparing, but he doesn't feel hungry, he's too anxious about what he's going to do. He's going to telephone the big house where Harriet lived until she married and went to live in the West Country. Though Major Cavanagh and his wife will be old, Micky senses that people who live comfortably live long and he feels certain that when the receiver is picked up it will be one of them who answers. And he knows exactly what he will say, he's prepared it. "You won't remember me, Major, but I'm an old friend of Harriet's and would very much like to get in touch…"

There's a payphone near the draughty front door of the guest house. Micky arranges 10p coins in a pile on top of it and searches in the local directory for the number. It's there as he expected. Cavanagh, Major C.N.H., High House, Matchford.

He takes a deep breath. His landlady has a television in her kitchen and music and laughter from a comedy show are blaring out.

Micky presses the receiver tight to his ear and tries to shut out the noise. He dials the number. He hears it ring six times before it's picked up and a voice he remembers as Mrs Cavanagh's says graciously, "Matchford two one five."

"Mrs Cavanagh," Micky begins, after pressing in the first of the coins, "you won't remember me, but -"

"This isn't Mrs Cavanagh," says the voice, "Will you hold on and I'll get her."

"Harriet?" says Micky.

There's a pause. Micky reaches out and holds on tightly to the top of the payphone box.

"Yes. Who is this?"

Another pause. The laughter from the landlady's TV is raucous.

"Sorry. Who?"

"Micky Stone. You probably won't remember me. I used to live with my mother in Slate Cottage."

"Oh yes. I remember you. Micky Stone. Gosh."

"I didn't think you'd be here, Harriet. I was going to ask where you were so that I could ring you up and talk to you."

"Were you? Heavens. What about?"

Another burst of laughter comes out of the kitchen. Micky covers his left ear with his hand. "I hadn't planned what about. About the old days, or something. About your pony."

"Golly yes. I remember. You used to stand at the gate…"

"Wait!" says Micky. "Can you wait a moment? Can you hang on?"

"Yes. All right. Why?"

"Hang on, please Harriet. I'll only be a minute."

Micky feeds another 10p coin into the pay slot, then runs as fast as he can up the stairs to his room. He grabs the tape machine and the microphone and hurtles down again. His landlady opens her kitchen door and stares as he rushes past. He picks up the telephone.

The recorder is on and turning, the little mike held against Micky's head.

"Harriet? Are you still there?"

A pause. Micky hears the door of the kitchen close.

"Yes."

"So you remember me at the gate?"

"Yes…"

"I once helped whitewash your stable and the dairy…"

"Yes. Lucky."

"What?"

"Lucky. My little horse. He was called Lucky. My children have got ponies now, but they don't awfully care about them. Not like I cared about Lucky."

"You rode so well."

"Did I? Yes. I loved that, the early morning rides. Getting up in the dark. It was quite a long way to your lane. I think it'd usually be light, wouldn't it, by the time I came up there? I'd be boiling by that time, even in snowy weather. Terribly hot, but awfully happy. And I remember, if you weren't there sometimes, if you were working or having breakfast or something, I used to think it was rather a bad omen. I was so superstitious, I used to think the day would go badly or Lucky would throw me, or Mummy would be cross or something, and quite often it went like that—things did go wrong if I hadn't seen you. Isn't that stupid? I'd forgotten all that till I spoke to you, but that's exactly how it was. I suppose you could say you were my good luck charm. And actually, I've often thought about you and wondered how you'd got on. I was rather sad when they demolished Slate Cottage. Did you know they had? I remember thinking every bit of one's life has kind of landmarks and Slate Cottage was definitely a landmark for me and I don't like it that it's not there any more. But you knew it had gone, did you?"

"Not till today…"

"Oh, it went years ago. Like lots of things. Like Lucky and the morning rides. Horrid, I think. I hate it when things are over.

My marriage is over. That's why I'm staying here. So sad and horrid it's all been. It just makes me think—jolly stupidly, because I know one can never bring time back—but it does make me see that those days when I was growing up and you were my lucky charm were important. What I mean is, they were good."

★

Lying in bed, Micky waits till the house is quiet. Outside his window, the snow is falling again. When he switches on the recorder and listens to Harriet's voice, he realizes for the first time that he forgot to put in a new tape and that most of his work at the windmill is now obliterated. About a minute of it remains, however. As Harriet Cavanagh fades to silence, her words are replaced by the sound of the big sails going round and round.

This collection first published in 2010 by Full Circle Editions

Introduction © Rose Tremain 2010; *Peerless* © Rose Tremain 2005, from
The Darkness of Wallis Simpson and Other Stories (Hamish Hamilton); *Strawberry
Jam* © Rose Tremain 1987, from *The Garden of the Villa Mollini* (Chatto & Windus);
A Shooting Season © Rose Tremain 1984, from *The Colonel's Daughter and Other
Stories* (Hamish Hamilton); *Wildtrack* © Rose Tremain 1987, from *The Garden of
the Villa Mollini* (Chatto & Windus)

Images copyright © Jeff Fisher 2010
The moral right of the author and artist has been asserted.

Design and Layout © Full Circle Editions 2010
Parham House Barn, Brick Lane, Framlingham, Woodbridge, Suffolk IP13 9LQ
www.fullcircle–editions.co.uk

A CIP record for this book is available from the British Library.

Set in Plantin Light & Gill Sans
Printed on Regent Kiara 135gsm from FSC Mixed Sources

Book design: Jonathan Christie

Printed and bound in Suffolk by Healeys Print Group, Ipswich

ISBN 978-0-95618-69-3-5

Note on the typeface:
Plantin Light is part of the Monotype Plantin family, a modern revival typeface
that was first cut in 1913. Its origins date back to the 16th century, specifically
to serif typefaces cut by Robert Granjon, and is named after Christophe Plantin
(1520—1589), an influential Renaissance humanist, book printer and publisher.
It is one of the typefaces that influenced the creation of Times Roman and today
features a full suite of small caps, ligatures and old style figures.

LOTTERY FUNDED